Praise for *Bigfoot Threw Rocks at Me (So I F*cked It)*

'I see you wrote a book instead of going to therapy.'
Author's Best Friend

'I dunno, I thought it was kind of hot.'
Author's Other Friend

'As a piece of writing, *Bigfoot Threw Rocks at Me* soars to the level of mediocrity.'
A Famous Journalist, Probably

'Maybe it's the overuse of the word c*ck, or the obscenely ludicrous plot, but I thought this book was fantastic.'
Some Perve

About the Author

DANIELLE DEVOUR loves two things in this life: folklore and HP Lovecraft. After working for years as a ghostwriter, penning romance under the names of others, she decided to do it for herself. What transpired was a mash-up of spice, horror, and weird fiction.

BIGFOOT
THREW ROCKS AT ME (SO I F*CKED IT)

DANIELLE DEVOUR

veil and
vortex

Chapter One

My keys jingle as I unlock my front door. It's been a long day —
a long week even — but there's no time to rest. I have to pack
my bags and head out again almost immediately if I want to
reach the Payette National Forest before nightfall. Can't hunt
for Bigfoot in the dark!

The footprints that were found are astonishing. I'll need to
make casts of the prints first, and then I'll need to cross-reference
the stride length with the data I have from the— Rose petals?
Flickering candlelight? The smell of gourmet cooking?

My boots crunch on the trail of red petals leading from the
entrance toward the kitchen. What in the world? Did Mark do
this? Either that or I have a very romantic home intruder.

Dropping my backpack, I follow the petal path curiously.

"Mark? You home?" I call out, pushing open the door to the
kitchen.

He whips around from the stove, brow furrowing when he
sees me.

"Emily! You're back already?"

"Yeah, I just got in...."

My voice trails off as I take in the whole domestic scene — the candlelit table, the sizzling pans, the bouquet of roses as the centerpiece on the table.

"What's all this?"

Mark's shoulders slump.

"You forgot, didn't you?"

"Forgot wha—"

The realization smacks me. It's our fucking anniversary. I rake a hand through my hair as Mark nods sadly. Of course — tonight's the 22nd. Three years ago today I marched into his microbiology lab, ranting about potential sasquatch specimens, and somehow he asked me out instead of calling security.

Mark's frustration is palpable as he leans back against the counter, his voice tight.

"You forgot, didn't you? God damn it, Emily. What's your excuse this time?"

I wince, feeling the sting of his words.

"Mark, someone found new prints at the Payette National Forest. It's a big deal — bigger than we thought. I just got caught up in the excitement, you know?"

His gaze hardens, and he crosses his arms, shaking his head.

"You're always caught up in it. Sometimes I think you love that damn Bigfoot more than you love me."

He's being melodramatic again. Jesus Christ, here we go.

"That's ridiculous, Mark," I reply, trying my hardest not to roll my eyes.

"Is it?" His voice rises slightly. "Think about it, Emily. How many dinners have you missed? How many nights have you come home late or not at all because you were out chasing some lead? How many trips have we had to cancel because new evidence has come in?"

Each question hits like a dart. In some ways, he's not wrong. I *do* put my research first, but can you blame me? Mark isn't leaving mysterious footprints and then disappearing off into the woods never to be seen again. I *have* to prioritize Bigfoot or we'll never catch him.

I reach for his hand, trying to bridge the gap between us.

"Mark, hunting Bigfoot isn't like other jobs. I can't just put it on pause. When evidence comes in, I have to act immediately. You know that my job is important to me."

He pulls his hand away gently. He looks tired.

"I get that it's important to you, Emily. I do. But I need to feel like I'm important too."

I sigh. This old argument again.

"You *are* important to me, Mark."

Mark's frustration is clear as he steps back, putting physical distance between us.

"Am I? We've been together three years, Emily. And sometimes it feels like you're somewhere else, with your thoughts, your plans... Always looking for the next clue, the next expedition."

Come on Emily. Don't lose your temper. Don't lose your temper. Just take a deep breath.

"Mark, we moved in together. Isn't that serious enough? Doesn't that say something about how much I care?"

He gives me a small, sad smile.

"Moving in is one thing, Em, but how often do we actually see each other? How many evenings do you spend out there instead of here with me?"

His voice carries a weariness that tugs at my heart. Maybe he's right, maybe I have been neglecting him. When did we last have sex? I don't remember. Jeez. Has it been that long?

I think back to the day we met. I crashed into his department at the university like a hurricane. Picture this: me, wildly gesticulating with a cooler in hand, inside of which was what I solemnly declared to be Bigfoot scat. I was all fired up, practically demanding someone analyze it immediately. Mark was the lone brave soul who didn't eye the door when I started my rant. Instead of calling security, which let's be honest, would have been reasonable, he just raised an eyebrow and said, *Slow down. I'll look at your sample, but you owe me a coffee if I'm touching that thing.* And just like that, he became my unexpected anchor in a sea of academic skeptics. He actually did analyze the sample. It turned out to be a weird bear-deer poop cocktail. Go figure.

Mark exhales heavily. Some of the tension leaves his face. Maybe the argument is over.

"Can we just not argue tonight? Can't we just try to enjoy what's left of our anniversary?" he asks, gesturing to the carefully laid table.

Fuck. I just realized I haven't told him I'm leaving tonight for the expedition. The argument is *not* over, it's only just begun.

Mark's expression shifts as he watches me, a crease forming between his brows. He can always tell when something's on my mind.

"What is it, Emily? What are you not telling me?"

I pause, steeling myself against the war I'm about to unleash.

"I... I have to go away for the weekend."

The confession hangs in the air, too heavy, too harsh for the soft candlelight. His face falls immediately, and the small flicker of hope that maybe we could salvage the evening extinguishes.

"Away? Now? But you just got in."

"It's the footprints," I rush to explain, my words tumbling out in a desperate flurry. "It's this big opportunity to gather evidence, and I can't miss it. I have to leave tonight."

Mark clenches his fists and for a moment I think he's going to punch something.

"Tonight? You're leaving tonight, on our anniversary, after all this?" he asks incredulously. He motions around to the romantic setup now tinged with irony.

I flinch, realizing how selfish my plans must seem.

"I'm sorry, Mark. I didn't plan for it to happen like this—"

"But it always does, doesn't it?" His words are sharp. They slice through the tense air. "It always does, Emily. There's always something more important."

I stand there, unable to find the words to soothe or explain further. I can see the pain etched in his eyes and yet, I'm not changing my mind. I'm leaving tonight.

Mark's frustration boils over, his voice rising to fill the space between us,

"You're chasing a fairytale, Emily! And all the while your prince charming is right here!"

I literally cannot stop myself from laughing. What a stupid statement.

"Stop being such a wet blanket, Mark! Prince Charming, my ass."

He reels back as if I've slapped him, his eyes flashing with hurt.

"At least I'm real, Emily! Unlike Bigfoot!"

Oh no. He did not just say that.

"How dare you!" I say through a clenched jaw.

But Mark isn't listening anymore. He's already moving away, his movements sharp and quick as he grabs his coat from the hook in the hall. He pauses at the front door, his hand on the knob. Tension lines his shoulders.

"I'm going to a bar, and I'll see you when you get back."

His words are clipped, final. Without waiting for a response, he pulls open the door and steps out. The cool night air sweeps in briefly as the door slams shut behind him.

Well, that could have gone better...

I sink into a chair, my thoughts swirling chaotically. I feel bad for Mark. It's hard being in love with a wild thing. You try to hold on, to find stability, but you're always chasing something elusive, something just out of reach. I should know — I've built my career on chasing wild things.

As I sit alone, the reality of the evening's disaster settles in. Mark is gone. The room is silent. Methodically, I turn off the stove, the soft clicks echoing louder than usual in the empty kitchen. The sizzle of the dinner simmers into silence.

I head upstairs. In my room, I grab my duffel bag from the closet and toss in clothes and necessities. Once packed, I haul the bag down the stairs and out the front door. My campervan sits in the driveway. My steadfast companion, always ready for the next adventure. It's stocked with gear, maps, and enough provisions to last several days in the isolation of the forest.

Climbing into the driver's seat, I start the engine. The familiar rumble is a soothing balm to my frazzled nerves. As I pull away from the house, the street lights flicker overhead, casting shadows that dance across the dashboard.

A weekend apart will be good for both Mark and me. Maybe some space will clear our heads, mend the rifts. After all, they say absence makes the heart grow fonder, right? And if it doesn't? Well, maybe I'll meet a nice, rugged mountain man in a checkered shirt. Someone who understands the call of the wild. Someone as untamed as the myths I chase.

Chapter Two

The road twists deeper into the Payette National Forest, each turn drawing me further away from my life's chaos. Away from Mark. The forest grows denser, a lush canopy knitting tightly above. The evening light filters through leaves in dappled patterns. It's beautiful and alien, like stepping into a parallel world where my problems can't quite reach me.

I've driven this path before, many times, chasing shadows and footprints. But tonight, there's a flutter in my stomach, a whisper in the back of my mind: *This time will be different. I can feel it. I'm going to find Bigfoot.*

Pulling into my usual camping area, I kill the engine and step out into the twilight. The air is crisp, filled with the sharp scent of pine and earth. The immediate drop in temperature makes me shiver. The familiar sounds of the forest at night greet me — crickets chirping, the occasional rustle of small creatures in the underbrush, the distant call of an owl. This place is more home to me than my house with Mark ever is.

I get to work, my movements automatic. First, I secure the area, checking for signs of recent animal activity. I don't need a bear wandering through tonight. Next, I pop open the back of the campervan, pulling out my portable kitchen. It's nothing fancy — just a small stove and a cooler packed with provisions — but it's enough. I set up a foldable table and chair. My little enclave where I can jot down notes and refuel with a hot meal. Once that's done, I prepare my research equipment. Night vision goggles, audio recorders, and plaster for footprint casts. I line them up neatly on another table, my outdoor lab under the stars. I've learned the hard way that being organized out here makes all the difference.

As the shadows stretch and the sky deepens to a dark blue, the whole forest comes alive with noise. Crickets get their groove on, squirrels scamper home, and possums make a late-night booty call. At least someone is getting laid tonight...

It's getting cold. The chill of the evening sneaks through my jacket, so I zip it up all the way, watching my breath fog up in front of me. I sweep the beam of my flashlight around, making the shadows jump. It's too dark to do any investigating tonight. I should probably head to bed.

I shuffle into the campervan, feeling the cool night air nipping at my heels as I close the door behind me. The routine is simple — brush my teeth, change into some comfy pajamas, and pull down the small bed. It's surprisingly cozy in here, even with the drop in temperature. I'm usually knocked out the minute my head hits the pillow. But not tonight. Tonight, my mind races.

I roll over, adjusting my position, trying to find that sweet spot on the cool side of the pillow. But it's not working.

Come on Emily. Just sleep. It must be my argument with Mark still playing in my subconscious. Twat. Even out here, he's ruining my calm.

Eventually, after what feels like hours of battling with my thoughts, my body succumbs to sleep. My eyes finally close, my mind slowly quiets, and then the dreams come...

Chapter Three

I am standing in a clearing in the forest. The night air is still and quiet, with only the soft chirping of crickets in the distance. Looking down, I realize I'm wearing a sheer, white dress. The material is soft and light, fluttering lightly in the breeze. I am naked underneath. My nipples stand to attention in the night air.

All around me in the clearing, candles flicker in glass jars. Their flames dance and send shadows across the grass and trees. The candles form a large circle around where I stand, their warm glow the only light in this serene place. It's peaceful here. Where am I?

I close my eyes and breathe deeply, taking in the earthy scents of pine and moss. I can feel the soft grass beneath my bare feet, the caress of the dress against my skin, the gentle wind through my hair.

I hear a sound and open my eyes. Someone is here.

A man emerges from the darkness. He is tall and broad. His rugged, handsome features come into the flickering candlelight as he steps into the clearing. He wears jeans slung low on his hips. I can see a peek of hair just above his belt, disappearing under his shirt. He wears a checkered shirt, unbuttoned halfway to reveal his muscular chest underneath.

I inhale sharply at the sight of this masculine stranger. He moves with a relaxed confidence and seems completely at ease. As he approaches me, his eyes lock intensely on mine. I am powerless under his piercing gaze. My heart is beginning to race.

When he reaches me, he extends his hand. I place my trembling fingers in his strong grip. Without a word, he pulls me against his hard body and begins to slow-dance with me there under the stars. I melt into his embrace, my breasts pressed to his chest, our hips swaying together. His hands explore the curve of my back, fingers trailing over the thin fabric of my dress. I tangle my hands in his thick hair and breathe him in. He smells of pine and woodsmoke and something entirely primal.

The man pulls me even closer as we dance, his strong arms wrapped tightly around my waist. His hand slides up my back and grasps the nape of my neck firmly, tilting my head back so I'm looking up into his eyes. They seem to glow amber in the candlelight.

Leaning down, he brushes his lips against mine in a feather-light kiss that sends a shiver through my entire body. I part my lips eagerly, wanting more, but he pulls back with a knowing smile. I whimper. I want him to kiss me, and he knows it.

The man leans in, claiming my mouth in a searing kiss. His tongue plunges between my lips as his hands grasp my backside, pulling my hips hard against the growing bulge in his jeans. I moan into his mouth, consumed with desire.

My dream lover lays me down on the soft grass, but he remains standing. He turns away to remove his clothes. As he slips off his shirt, the muscles along his broad back flex and ripple. He unbuckles his belt slowly. Finally, he slides his jeans down, revealing muscular thighs and firm buttocks. When he turns back, he is changed. His body is now covered in dark, coarse hair from head to toe. His hands have grown larger, the fingers extended into claws. His face has elongated into a snout, with sharp fangs peeking from his mouth. He lets out a low, rumbling growl that vibrates through my body. I gasp as I realize this is no ordinary man, but the legendary Bigfoot himself.

Bigfoot moves toward me on all fours, his amber eyes burning with animal passion. I know I should run, but I can't. I am frozen in place, my heart hammering in my chest.

My eyes are drawn to the massive bulge between his hairy thighs. It growls — twitching and pulsing as if it has a mind of its own. It extends. It snakes its way around my body, encircling me like a living, throbbing cage. It slithers up my thighs, teasing my aching entrance with its velvety softness.

The immense girth of Bigfoot's cock presses against my pussy lips. I can feel the heat emanating from it. His amber eyes lock onto mine as he begins to push forward, the tip of his thick member breaching me ever so slightly. The flared head of his massive cock spreads me wide.

I scream in pleasure and pain. I want him but I can barely take it. He'll rip me open if he goes any further. But by God, do I want him to rip me open.

Chapter Four

I jolt awake, heart pounding. I sit up abruptly, my eyes darting around in the dim light. Where are the trees, the candles? Oh, right. It was just a dream.

I blink, scanning the corners of the campervan, half-expecting to see flickering light or the towering figure of Bigfoot lingering by the door. But there's nothing. Just the usual clutter of my gear and the soft hum of the forest outside. No candles. No Bigfoot. Just me.

I rub my eyes, letting out a long breath. Get a grip, Emily.

Reaching between my legs, I find I'm dripping wet. My inner thighs are slick with arousal. Slowly, I lie back down, the bed creaking softly under my weight. I pull the blanket up to my chin, determined to find sleep again, but the sun is beginning to rise. I guess I'm getting up then.

I slide out of bed, still shaking off the remnants of the dream. I need coffee, badly. I unpack my little kitchen out the back of the campervan and get the stove going. The familiar hiss of the burner is comforting, and soon, the aroma of coffee fills the air. While the coffee brews, I rummage through my provisions for something to eat. Breakfast is simple — a granola bar and an apple. Nothing fancy, but it does the trick.

With my steaming mug in hand, I settle into a camping chair and pull out my phone.

Hmm, two messages from Mark. The first one is an apology, and the second one is asking if I arrived ok. I should probably reply. But I'm not going to. Not yet anyway. Let him worry.

I lock the phone and set it aside, focusing on my coffee instead. The warmth of the drink soothes me, the bitterness sharp and grounding. Grounding is good. I need grounding after that weird dream.

I finish my coffee and stare out into the vast, awakening forest. Time to get moving. There's a lot to do today.

The forest is crisp, the morning air sharp with the eye-opening scent of pine and earth. I pull on my backpack and adjust the straps, ensuring it's snug against my shoulders. Stepping off the well-worn trail, I venture deeper into the less-trodden areas of the Payette National Forest. Here, the signs of human passage fade and the true wild begins to unfold.

Around me, the forest is alive with the subtle grandeur of nature untouched. Tall pines tower overhead, their canopies interlocking to create a mosaic of green and gold as the sunlight filters through. Each step I take is cushioned by the mix of soft loam and scattered pine needles beneath me. Every breath I take feels like a gulp of pure, cold water — refreshing and invigorating.

Small ferns and wildflowers peek through the underbrush, dotting the landscape with splashes of color. Whites, yellows, and the vibrant greens that only appear in the deep woods. Occasionally, a bird flits by in a flash of color, its song a fleeting melody quickly swallowed by the vastness of the forest. Every so often, I pause to listen. I let the forest's rhythm sync with my heartbeat. I am exactly where I belong. Here, I am just another creature in the forest, tracing the footsteps of legends and beasts.

After trudging around for what feels like forever, I finally find the Bigfoot print. And let me tell you, it's a whopper. Deep, unmistakable. I can barely contain my excitement as I crouch down for a closer look. This is seriously fucking amazing.

This footprint is massive — my entire shoe could fit in it twice over. The toes are all splayed out, and you can really see the definition like it just stepped there moments ago. And the heel part? Even deeper. This Bigfoot must be huge. It's been snacking well out here, that's for sure.

I whip out my tape measure and start measuring like a detective at a crime scene. I'm talking length, width, and depth. I scribble everything into my notebook, feeling a bit like a kid logging her most epic find yet in her diary. Then, it's photo time. I snap pictures from every angle imaginable. Including a few selfies. Mark is not going to believe this!

Shit. Mark. I didn't text him back. I'm sure he's worried but he'll have to wait. This is too important to ignore and Mark will still be at the end of the phone in an hour from now.

Grinning ear to ear, I mix up the plaster. The mixture has to be just right. Too runny, and it won't capture the fine details. Too thick, and it could distort them. This print is going to make an awesome cast if I can get the mixture right.

I pour in the plaster, watching it settle into all the nooks and crannies. Every time I do this, it's like I'm unlocking a little piece of the mystery — getting one step closer to proving everyone who doubted me wrong. And let me tell you, that feels pretty darn good.

Ok, now I have to wait for it to set. The plaster will be touch dry in about ten minutes. I'll take a look around for any other evidence while I wait.

I wander away from the print, keeping my eyes peeled. Normally, the forest just feels like... well, forest. Trees, bushes, the usual suspects. But here, around where I found the footprint, the air feels charged. Almost buzzing. It's like someone's rubbed a balloon on my hair. Something about this particular spot feels off. It's not just the eerie stillness or the way sounds seem muffled here — it's as if the very air is heavy, holding its breath.

Shit. What if it's the Elementals? The last time I was here, I stopped at a gas station just outside Payette and this indigenous elder told me a story about forest spirits. Elementals he called them. He said that the air feels electric and then they come for you, whisking you away, never to be seen again. I know it sounds crazy, but so does Bigfoot to most people.

I let out a sharp breath and shake my arms, trying to expel my nerves. Get it together Emily.

This is when I see them — broken branches. These aren't your average twiggy branches; these are big, hefty ones. Snapped clean off about seven feet up the tree. No storm did this — storms don't pick and choose that neatly. And it's not a bear either. They climb, sure, but snapping branches like these clean off? Unlikely.

I circle the tree, peering up into the canopy and then back down at the forest floor, looking for any signs of what could have done this. The breaks are fresh, the wood inside still pale and not yet darkened by exposure.

I pull out my camera to take a few photos. Every bit of evidence adds up, paints a bigger picture. And this picture? It's starting to get really interesting.

Leaning in closer to the broken branches, my eyes catch a glimpse of something tangled in the rough bark. Fur! Not just a few strands, but a good clump.

"Hello, what have we got here?" I whisper to myself.

I pull out my tweezers and a plastic bag from my backpack, the tools of the trade for a careful collection. I'm gentle as I tease the fur away from the bark. Bringing the fur close to my nose, I take a cautious sniff. It's musky, wild, and distinctly animal — unlike anything I typically encounter. Not deer, definitely not bear. Something else. Could this be Bigfoot fur?

"I wish you could talk and tell me your story," I say to the fur, half-joking.

Securing the fur in the bag, I press out the air, seal it tight, and stash it in my backpack. This little bit of mystery fur could be the piece of evidence that ties everything together, or it might just raise more questions. Either way, I can't wait to find out!

With the fur safely tucked into my backpack, I pause to sweep my gaze across the surrounding area again. I don't want to miss anything else.

Why does it feel like the forest is watching me? What's out there?

Suddenly, a sharp crack behind me shatters the eerie calm. I spin around, my heart hammering in my ears. My eyes dart frantically, searching through the dim shadows cast by the towering trees. My hand shakes as I reach for the bear repellent strapped to my belt.

"Who's there?" I call out, as if that's going to deter a bear from eating my face.

As the seconds stretch out and nothing attacks, my racing heart starts to slow. I keep the repellent close though — I'm not ready to let my guard down yet. Whatever made that sound could still be close, watching, calculating.

I glance at my watch. Three hours back to camp. With the sun already dipping toward the horizon and that unsettling crack in the trees, it's best I don't waste any time. I need to make it back before dark. No telling what's out here with me.

I crouch down next to the plaster cast of the footprint. It's hard to the touch now, set enough to travel. Carefully, I slide my hands underneath it, lifting it from the mud. It's heavier than it looks but I'll be able to manage.

I pull out the roll of bubble wrap from my backpack and wrap the cast meticulously. It's precious cargo — the kind of evidence that makes or breaks careers. Once secure, I tuck it into my backpack.

"Alright, let's get moving," I mutter to myself, scanning the surrounding trees one last time. The forest seems to have returned to normal, the earlier tension has lifted. The static feeling has gone. Weird.

The walk back is brisk, my steps quick and purposeful. I keep my ears tuned to any sounds, my hand never straying far from the bear repellent. Every rustle in the underbrush, every snap of a twig sends a shot of adrenaline through me. But the path is clear, I'll be back soon.

As I push through the last stretch of dense foliage, I see the outline of my campervan in the fading light. I've made it, thank fuck.

Chapter Five

It's after dinner. I'm rinsing my plate, the last remnants of my meal being washed off into the brush of the forest. My feet ache from the day's trek, and honestly, all I can think about is crawling into my campervan and losing myself in a book before sleep. Just a regular night. No weird dreams.

I fold up my little kitchen, tucking everything neatly into the back of the van. Efficiency is key out here; everything has its place.

I'm rounding the van to the side door, my thoughts already drifting to which book I'll read tonight. But then, a sound stops me cold. It's a series of deep, guttural grunts that cut through the quiet night. I freeze, straining my ears.

That sound... It's not an animal. At least, I hope it's not. But it's definitely not human either. What *is* it? It couldn't be...? Could it?

I stand there for a second, debating. Curiosity wars with the sensible urge to jump into the van and lock the door. But I know myself better than that — I need to know what's making that noise.

Taking a deep breath, I step away from the safety of the van. My hand clutches the flashlight, but I don't dare use it. Whatever it is, I don't want it to know I'm coming.

I creep slowly through the dark forest, moving as quietly as I can over the crackling underbrush. The strange grunts and groans seem to be coming from just up ahead, beyond a thick copse of trees. A chill runs down my spine, but I can't turn back now. I have to know what's making those unearthly sounds.

I pause behind a wide fir tree and peer around it cautiously. There, in a moonlit clearing, stands two hulking figures, far larger than any human. I freeze, my breath catching in my throat. It's not one, but two Bigfoot. I've dreamed of this moment for years and now it's finally here.

My hand instinctively goes to the camera bag on my hip before I remember that I left it behind in the van. Of all the nights to be unprepared! No one will ever believe me.

Careful not to make a sound, I inch further around the fir tree for a better view. The Bigfoot faces are human-like, with wise, old eyes. The larger one grooms the smaller, picking at its fur with unexpected tenderness.

Should I stay? What if they spot me, or hear me? If I startle them, who knows how they'll react...

The two beasts continue their low grunting, seemingly unaware of my presence. I know I should creep away quietly before they notice me, but I'm transfixed. This is a once-in-a-lifetime chance to observe these elusive creatures up close. I'm not going to waste it.

The two Bigfoot continue to groom one another, the smaller of the two grunts and nuzzles into the bigger one. This is incredible. Maybe it's a courting ritual.

The smaller Bigfoot gets down on its hands and knees, and the larger one walks behind him. He's carrying a thick branch.

Oh god, wait. That's not a branch. That's his cock. Holy shit, it's huge!

I watch in horror and fascination as the larger of the two begins to slide his mammoth cock inside the ass of the smaller one. How do I know it's in the ass? Because the smaller Bigfoot appears to have a fucking massive branch between his legs too!

I gasp in shock, unable to look away as the larger one mounts the smaller one. Their guttural grunts take on a new, urgent tone that sends a flush of heat through my body.

Should I leave? No. This is science. I am the only person to ever witness two Bigfoot mating. And two *males* at that!

I watch, mesmerized by the raw sensuality of their coupling. The Bigfoot move together with a primal intensity, the larger one's powerful body enveloping its partner. It's strangely beautiful, and as the beasts find their pleasure, I feel my own starting to build.

The smaller one grunts and pants, pushing back eagerly against its partner's powerful thrusts. Their fur glistens in the moonlight as they move together faster and harder.

Overwhelmed with desire, I allow my hand to glide down towards my thighs. I unfasten the button on my jeans and carefully unzip them, trying not to make any noise. My fingers find the warm, slick folds between my thighs and I begin to pleasure myself. I match my movements to the rhythmic rocking of the creatures, circling and stroking in time with their urgent pace. Pressure builds within me and I lean back against a tree, letting the sensations wash over me.

What am I doing? This is insane. You can't wank off in the forest, only 10 meters away from two Bigfoot. And yet, I can't help myself. It's as though their primal energy is infecting me. With each powerful thrust they make, my fingers move faster against my aching core, needing more, wanting more. The forest around us feels alive. The air begins to tingle with static as their musky scents mingle with the earthy smell of the forest floor. My vision begins to blur, and I fall into a trance-like state, fixated on the carnal act playing out in front of me.

The smaller Bigfoot grunts with pleasure. His eyes roll back in ecstasy as he nears his climax. I can feel my own orgasm approaching too, teetering on the edge. My breaths come short and shallow now, my heart pounding in my ears like drums beating out an ancient rhythm.

With each powerful thrust, a deep-seated need begins to unfurl itself within me. My mind spins with forbidden fantasies — I envision myself in the place of the smaller Bigfoot, being dominated by that colossal, throbbing cock. My hands work faster, desperate to satisfy the mounting hunger that burns between my thighs. Slickness coats my fingers as I edge closer and closer to release.

The smaller one's cock, still rock-hard, twitches with each powerful drive of the larger one's hips. I can't believe the size of it — thicker than my forearm, and longer too! I could never take such a thick cock... Or could I?

In the interest of science, I pull down my jeans, squat, and insert four fingers inside myself, trying to mimic the girth of the mighty Bigfoot. The invasion feels exhilarating, dangerous yet thrilling all at once. I move my hand in and out of myself, mimicking the couple's primal rhythm.

The tightness of my pussy pushes my desire to an unbearable peak, and with a shuddering cry, I discover myself climaxing harder than I ever have before. The world around me spins as wave after wave of bliss washes over me. Gasping for air, I finally tear my eyes away from the scene in front of me. What have I just done? I'm horrified. I've never done anything like this before.

Shaking off the post-orgasmic haze, I hastily wipe my hand off and zip my jeans. I need to get out of here before they notice me. I back away from the clearing, making sure not to step on any twigs or branches that might give away my presence.

Back at the van, I slam the door shut and lean against it, trying to catch my breath. I can't believe what just happened. Not only did I witness two Bigfoot mating, but I also got off on it! What came over me? How could I lose control like that? I'm a professional, not a pervert.

Professional! Yes! I need to write down everything I saw (missing out the parts where I fisted myself into oblivion, of course).

With trembling hands, I snatch up my notebook from the passenger seat, flipping it open to a blank page. I scribble down every detail while it's still fresh, the pen scratching urgently against the paper.

Suddenly, there's a scraping sound, right outside the van — a deliberate, dragging noise. My breath catches in my throat. It's too purposeful, too close to be just another forest creature going about its night.

I freeze. My heart beats a frantic tattoo against my ribs.

Silence.

Then another scrape, closer this time, as if something is circling the van. Without warning, a dull thud resonates through the metal — a rock striking the side of the camper. It's clear now; whatever is out there, it's trying to get my attention — or get in.

Chapter Six

One minute I'm writing notes, the next the campervan starts to shake violently. The world suddenly lurches and I fall.

What the–?

I scramble to my knees, heart hammering. This isn't just a gust of wind; it feels like something is deliberately rocking the van.

Thud. Thud.

The entire van shudders with each heavy step outside.

No, no, no. Shit. The Bigfoot must have seen me.

I crawl toward the front of the van, to the compartment where I usually stash my flashlight. I need to see what's happening. I need light. But my fingers grasp at empty air. Right, the flashlight. I left it outside when I was perving on the Bigfoot. I'll call for help instead. The signal is plenty good enough. I'll call the forest patrol.

Another massive jolt sends my phone skittering across the floor. I lunge for it, just managing to wrap my fingers around the edge when the van rocks again, harder this time. The phone slips from my grasp and shoots under the driver's seat. Damn it!

Panic claws up my throat. I can hear my breath, fast and ragged, barely audible over the sounds of my pounding heart and the ominous thumping outside. Each thud against the van's sturdy frame feels like a countdown to something unknown.

I'm on my hands and knees now, trying to reach my phone. The van tilts, everything goes sideways, and I'm thrown against the wall. Cans and utensils clatter around me. I need to get to my phone, I need to call for help — someone, anyone. But as I stretch my hand further under the seat, the van gives one violent heave, and I'm tossed back, my head hitting the floor. Or the wall. I don't know anymore. The van has completely gone over. The world spins. I'm disoriented, scared. I brace for another impact, sure that the beast will continue to pummel the van.

There's the sound of screeching metal. I flinch, my ears ringing as the door of the campervan groans under an unimaginable force. It's a sound of destruction, of bending steel and breaking hinges. A loud, horrific tearing that echoes through the forest like a cry of anger. With a final, deafening crack, the door gives way, ripped clean off its frame. It clatters to the ground outside, tossed aside as easily as a piece of aluminum foil.

The open doorway frames the night, a portal to my nightmare come alive. A giant hand reaches in. It's massive, with thick fingers and rough skin. The hand wraps around my arm. My heart skips. My stomach churns. I try to scream but it's nothing more than a whimper.

The grip tightens on my arm. It pulls. I resist, my other hand clutching anything within reach — the edge of a seat, the floor mat. But it's futile. The Bigfoot's strength is overwhelming, effortless. It pulls me from the van, and as it does, time seems to slow down. The air smells of pine and earth. The smell of its fur is musky and almost sweet. The hand that holds me is textured, the skin like old leather. Cool yet somehow alive with heat.

Leaves and twigs crunch under us as the Bigfoot pulls me along through the forest. Its massive strides are sure-footed and unhesitant, even in the dark. The ground is a blur of movement as we pass, the rustle of leaves loud under its heavy steps. My mind spins with fear, panic, and disbelief. My legs are unsteady, and I feel as though I may collapse at any moment. I try twisting my body in a desperate attempt to pull away, but the Bigfoot simply adjusts its grip.

"Please," I gasp, "please, don't hurt me."

My voice is breathless, tinged with desperation. The creature pauses, and for a moment, it looks at me. Then we're moving again. Branches scrape against my clothes. The night air whips my face. Every shadow in the forest seems to watch, every rustle a witness to my abduction. My body trembles, not just from fear, but from the cold realization of my utter helplessness.

As we continue through the forest, a strange calm settles over me. My thoughts are clear. I'm about to die. This is it. And strangely, I'm not thinking about Mark. I'm not worrying about us, or feeling guilty. We're over, and I'm ok with that. My life's work was to find Bigfoot. To prove they're real. And here I am, in the grip of one. I've done it. I've actually done it. Despite the terror, a weird pride swells in me. I smile, just a little. It's a bizarre feeling, being proud while being dragged to your death. I won't fight it. What will be will be.

My legs are weak. My head spins. The forest blurs around me, a mix of shadow and moonlight. I can barely keep my eyes open.

"I found you," I whisper to the night, to Bigfoot, to myself. My voice is a breath, lost in the rustle of the leaves.

And then everything goes black. My body gives out. I'm fainting, sinking into darkness with the knowledge that I've achieved what I set out to do. My quest is complete, right here in the unforgiving embrace of the unknown.

Chapter Seven

I start to wake. Without opening my eyes I roll over in my bed. My dream had seemed so real. The shaking of the van and the sound of ripping metal. I need to stop eating cheese before bed.

My hand reaches out for the duvet, but it's not there. Wait. Where am I?

Confused, I open my eyes and sit up quickly, a light panic setting in. The memories flood back — being dragged from the campervan, the massive hand gripping my arm. It wasn't a dream.

I blink and look around. Where am I? It looks like I'm in some kind of rudimentary four-poster bed. The posts are rough, made from branches, and the mattress is a surprisingly soft layer of moss. Vines, twisted and braided, form makeshift curtains around the bed. My heart pounds as I take in my surroundings. The space is dimly lit but warm. I can hear the crackle of a fire nearby. This isn't home. This isn't the campervan either.

I breathe deeply, trying to calm myself. The earthy smell of the moss and the faint smoke from the fire fills my senses. This isn't what I expected from a kidnapping by Bigfoot.

I listen closely. There's nothing but the crackling of the fire. No footsteps, no strange noises. Just the fire.

I move to the edge of the bed, my heart still racing, and tentatively peek through the vine curtains. The fire's glow casts flickering shadows on the walls. It's a cave. It has to be.

I pull back the vines further, revealing more of the room. The walls are rough stone, cool and damp. The fire sits in a small pit, surrounded by rocks. There are a few makeshift shelves, carved directly into the rock, holding what looks like bundles of herbs and other natural supplies. Is this a bedroom?

I stand up slowly, leaving the safe haven of the bed. I look up and see the cave ceiling soaring high above me. It's dark, with no hint of daylight peeping through. How deep underground am I?

My curiosity pushes my fear aside. I take a few steps into the room, the fire's warmth on my back. This place is incredible, but also unnerving. The silence is profound, the isolation complete. I glance around the cave again, taking in the details. The bed is surprisingly comfortable, and the warmth from the fire is soothing. Oddly, I'm not particularly scared. You'd think I would be, but instead, my scientific brain is in overdrive, trying to absorb every detail.

Shit, what's that noise?

I turn and see a Bigfoot emerge from an entrance I hadn't noticed before. My heart skips a beat, but I don't run or scream. Instead, I watch.

The Bigfoot is massive, its fur a deep brown with a distinctive striped pattern running down its arms. The stripes are almost like a natural camouflage, blending with the shadows of the cave. I need to keep a mental note of everything I see down here — a catalog of Bigfoot fur patterns would be a fascinating read for any Sasquatch fan.

The creature sees me. It pauses, then approaches slowly, carefully, like it doesn't want to scare me. In its hands, the Bigfoot carries something wrapped in leaves. It stops a few feet from the fire and places the bundle gently on the ground. Then, in a movement that almost makes me gasp, it bows slightly toward me before retreating to the entrance.

Bows? Did it just show me some kind of respect or reverence?

I stand there, processing what just happened. Stripe, as I decide to call him, because of the striped pattern on its arms, clearly doesn't mean any harm. Instead, there's a gentleness in his actions, a deliberate attempt to communicate.

I move closer to the fire and inspect the bundle Stripe left. The leaves are neatly wrapped, and inside, I find some kind of cooked meat. My stomach growls, reminding me that I'm hungry. I take a tentative bite. It's delicious, rich and smoky. This is amazing — Bigfoot room service.

Finishing the food, I sit back down on the mossy bed. What do I do now? Stripe's behavior suggests intelligence and social structure — traits I hadn't dared to hope for. The fire's warmth and the comfortable bed make it clear that they want me to feel safe, maybe even welcome. Perhaps I am not a kidnapped human, but a guest.

I glance toward the entrance where Stripe had disappeared. Do I follow him? I can either stay here and wait for another Bigfoot to enter, or I can explore. Staying put feels safe, but also passive. I'd just be waiting for something to happen. Exploring though? That could lead to danger. If these Bigfoot are hostile, I might get killed or eaten. But surely that would have happened by now... Worst case scenario: I die. Best case scenario: they're friendly and I convince one to come back to civilization with me. Shit. Imagine that!

My curiosity wins out. I need to know more. I stand up from the bed, feeling a mix of excitement and nervousness. This is what I've always dreamed of — real, firsthand discovery.

"Alright, Emily, let's do this," I whisper to myself, heading towards the entrance where Stripe came from.

I carefully peek around the corner of the entrance, expecting to be met with pitch darkness. But to my surprise, there's light. The tunnel ahead is softly illuminated by some kind of bioluminescent moss clinging to the walls. I smile and laugh to myself — it's beautiful, almost magical.

I step into the glowing tunnel. The soft light bathes everything in an ethereal glow, casting gentle shadows and making the stone walls look alive. As I walk down the rough corridor, my fingers brush the moss-covered walls. The texture is soft, almost velvety. This place is beyond anything I ever imagined. I wonder if this cave system is natural, or if the Bigfoot carved it somehow. The walls are rough, with natural formations that suggest a long history of geological activity. But some areas seem too smooth, too deliberate, as if shaped by intelligent hands. It's hard to tell for sure.

I don't have to walk far before I see a Bigfoot ahead. His colossal form blocks my path. He's facing away from me, but there's no getting past without him noticing. This is it — death time. He'll either let me pass, or chase me back up the tunnel and murder me. No point fighting the inevitable.

I cough politely like I'm trying to get the attention of a receptionist at the dentist's office.

"Um, excuse me?"

The Bigfoot turns around. It's Stripe again. He cocks his head to the side like a quizzical puppy. He looks confused to see me.

"Hey, Stripe," I say, stepping closer. "Where am I?"

I realize it's silly to speak to him like this. There's no way he'll understand me. But his facial expressions change, like he's actually trying to work out what I said. Then, to my surprise, he steps aside, clearing the path.

"Thanks," I mutter, amazed.

I walk past him but stop short. Ahead of me is a maze of caves and tunnels, branching off in all directions. I have no idea where to go. I turn back to Stripe.

"I don't know where to go," I admit, feeling a bit foolish.

He seems to understand. With a slow, deliberate movement, he gestures down a particular tunnel.

"Alright, lead the way," I say, even though he's not moving. I take the first step down the indicated tunnel, glancing back to make sure he's watching. He is. He follows slowly behind me, those intelligent eyes watching my every move.

Eventually, the tunnel opens into a larger chamber, filled with more bioluminescent moss. In the center, there's a pool of clear water, reflecting the soft light. The air is cool and damp, but not unpleasant. It feels like a sacred place, untouched and serene. I look around, awe-struck. The bioluminescent moss casts a soft, greenish glow, giving the chamber an otherworldly feel. The walls are dotted with clusters of glowing fungi and delicate, luminescent plants. The air is rich with the earthy scent of damp stone and a faint, sweet aroma. The pool itself is crystal clear, the water reflecting the glowing moss and creating a shimmering effect that dances across the ceiling.

"This is amazing," I whisper, not really expecting a response. But Stripe steps forward, his massive form surprisingly gentle as he moves. He points to the pool, then to his mouth. It takes me a second to understand.

"You want me to drink?"

He nods, or at least, I think that's what he's doing. I kneel by the pool and scoop up some water in my hand. It's cold and fresh, the cleanest water I've ever tasted.

"Thank you," I say.

Stripe watches me, his expression softening. For a moment, we just stand there, two beings from different worlds, finding a way to understand each other.

Stripe gestures again to the pool, and I shake my head slightly. "No, thanks. I've had enough to drink."

He makes a series of grunts and noises, his gestures becoming more animated. I tilt my head, trying to decipher his meaning. What's he trying to say?

Stripe moves to the edge of the pool, dips his hand in, and then pours the water over his arm. Suddenly, it clicks.

"Oh, you're offering me a bath?"

I frown, glancing at the pool, then down at my clothes. I take a tentative sniff. Yep, I probably do need a wash. It's been a couple of days since I've had a proper bath, and the thought of cleaning up is more appealing than I'd like to admit.

"Okay," I say, nodding slowly. "I guess a bath isn't a bad idea."

Stripe stands by the pool, watching me with those intelligent eyes. He seems almost proud of his offering, as if he's sharing a special part of his world with me.

"Thanks, Stripe," I say, smiling at him. The cave, with its glowing moss and serene pool, feels like a hidden gem. Who knew Bigfoot could be so thoughtful?

I can't help but chuckle at the situation. Here I am, deep in an underground cave, taking hygiene advice from a Bigfoot.

Slowly, I slip out of my hiking boots and socks, wiggling my toes in relief. My pants and underwear follow until I stand naked under the soft glow of the bioluminescent moss.

I feel Stripe's eyes on me, and a flush creeps up my cheeks that has nothing to do with the chill. I have never been shy about my body, but something about his steady gaze makes me suddenly self-conscious. Can a beast truly appreciate a woman's form? I shake the thought from my mind and dip a toe into the pool. Unable to resist, I slide in up to my neck, letting the water envelop me. A contented sigh escapes my lips.

Stripe moves closer to the edge of the pool, watching me. He starts making noises that are almost musical, a series of low, melodic hums and trills. Is he singing?

The sound is strangely relaxing, blending perfectly with the tranquil ambiance of the cave. I close my eyes, letting the cool water and music wash over me. It feels like a lullaby, soothing and ancient.

Then I feel it — an electricity in the air. The static feeling again. I open my eyes and glance around. I know what that means. More Bigfoot are coming.

From an entrance hidden in the shadows, a second Bigfoot emerges. Then a third. I freeze, treading water in the middle of the pool as more immense, hairy forms lumber into the cavern. There must be at least six of them now, their eyes glinting in the mossy light as they gaze upon me.

A nervous thrill courses through me. I'm completely exposed, naked in this pool with a troop of powerful beasts surrounding me. Logically, I know I should feel afraid, but I sense no malice in these creatures as they watch me.

The Bigfoot begin to hum and rumble to one another in that strange, melodic language. The acoustics of the cave amplify the sound until it resonates through my body like a living thing. Goosebumps prickle my bare skin, and not because of the cool water. I close my eyes again, letting the sound wash over and through me. The resonance seems to echo in the deepest parts of my body. I feel my core tighten and throb. It's as though their singing has awoken something primal in me.

I open my eyes, trying to focus on the here and now, and not the sensations inside me. The Bigfoot continue their wordless song. Their voices weave intricate melodies, sometimes discordant, sometimes harmonious.

The largest of the beasts steps closer to the pool's edge. He is broad. Muscular. I can see his toned body through the swirls of his dark fur. Softly, he steps into the pool with me. His amber eyes lock with mine, and in their dark depths I see wisdom and longing.

The beast reaches out a massive hand and brushes his fingers ever so lightly over the surface of the pool. Ripples spread from his touch, lapping against my bare breasts. The water's caress makes me shiver with delight. This is no dumb beast. This is an intelligent being, communicating in the only way it knows how.

I meet his gaze steadily, reading his intent. He wants me to react. He is looking for connection, for permission to come closer. Perhaps we are not so different, human and beast. We all seek belonging, intimacy, the comfort of another's touch.

Slowly, I reach out my hand, watching for any sign of retreat. Finding none, I brush my fingertips along the surface of the pool, sending ripples dancing back toward the Bigfoot. He rumbles low in his throat, a primal purr of satisfaction.

I feel an intense charge in the air between us. My body is alive, every nerve ending tingling. Slowly, dreamily, I glide through the water until I'm right before him.

I look around at the other Bigfoot, standing around the edge of the pool. Their singing has changed. It's lower, more guttural. Their massive bodies sway as they chant, their eyes half-closed. I glance down and gasp as I see their huge, engorged cocks in their hands. They're masturbating, stroking themselves slowly as they look at me and their alpha.

I freeze, unsure what to do. This could be dangerous, being surrounded by such powerful, virile creatures in the grips of primal need. But I cannot deny the heat blooming between my legs either, the throbbing desire awakened by their earthy display.

I look down into the water and notice that the alpha is working his thick length also. His eyes burn into me and he grunts, thrusting his hips forward suggestively. I know he can smell my arousal, as can the others. It's driving them wild. Their massive penises are now fully erect, jutting out from their furry groins like rigid spears.

I meet the gaze of the beast before me, reading the longing in those ancient eyes. Slowly, I reach out and trail my fingers down his powerful furry chest. He shudders, a rumbling groan escaping his throat. I sense his cock twitching with pent-up desire. He groans and convulses, his seed spilling into the water.

As if on cue, the other Bigfoot also reach their climaxes, and a chorus of primal roars echo through the cavern. I instinctively shut my eyes as hot cum erupts from their massive cocks, show-ering me in thick ropes of sticky seed. It coats my naked body, sliding down my breasts and into the water. I gasp as some of it hits my face, marveling at the strange yet strangely arousing sensation. Then the floating seed around me begins to glow. The light starts as a soft shimmer but quickly intensifies, filling the entire pool with a radiant luminescence. I gasp, shielding my eyes from the brilliance. The glow is almost too bright, casting dancing reflections on the cave walls and ceiling. It's like being surrounded by liquid starlight semen.

As the light pulses around me, the orgasmic sounds from Bigfoot begin to calm. Their humming and trills fade into a gentle murmur. The air hums with electricity.

Slowly, the light begins to dim. I lower my hand cautiously, peeking through my fingers. The pool is still glowing, but now it's a soft, inviting light, illuminating the cave in a warm, mag-ical glow. I look around, eyes wide with wonder, taking in the transformed space.

I start to relax when suddenly, I hear a voice. It's low and sensual, reverberating through my mind.

The ritual is complete.

I freeze. The voice is inside my head, but it's not my own. It arrived in my mind without passing through my ears. My heart races as I turn to look at the alpha Bigfoot. His gaze is calm and focused on me.

The voice speaks again, but the alpha's mouth doesn't move.

Do not be afraid, human. It is I speaking, Kruk. The alpha of my species.

My eyes widen in disbelief. Telepathy? This is beyond anything I could have imagined. My scientific brain struggles to keep up with the wonderment and confusion flooding my senses.

"Kruk," I whisper, testing the name in my mouth. It feels strange, foreign, yet powerful. "You... you can speak to me?"

Yes. We are unable to communicate with your species through word alone. Now that you have partaken in our ritual, we can communicate with you through thought. Do not be alarmed. You are safe here.

I glance around at the other Bigfoot, who watch me with a mixture of curiosity and reverence. The glowing water, the singing, the cum — it was all part of this ritual.

"Why have you brought me here?" I ask, my voice trembling.

Everything will be revealed, Kruk replies.

He extends his hand, palm open and inviting. Tentatively, I reach out and take it, feeling the rough texture of his skin against mine.

Kruk leads me out of the pool, the water cascading off me in gentle waves. As I step out of the pool, the jizz that had spilled into the water is completely gone, as though it was never there at all.

Stripe stands nearby, holding some kind of towel. I cannot tell what it's made from, maybe animal fur? Stripe wraps the towel around me, his movements gentle and respectful. The towel is surprisingly soft and warm. I pull it tight around myself.

Kruk's voice comes again, reassuring and calm.

You have many questions. In time, all will be answered. For now, rest and know you are among friends. We have much to share with you.

I nod, still processing the magnitude of what is happening. This is beyond anything I could have ever imagined.

Stripe gently guides me back down the glowing tunnel towards my chamber. The soft bioluminescent light creates a serene path as we walk, the cave's magic still enveloping me. When we arrive back at the makeshift bedroom, the bed of moss and woven vines looks even more inviting now. I'm exhausted.

Stripe gestures for me to lay down, his eyes kind and watchful. I slip under the mossy covers, feeling the day's events weighing heavily on me. The warmth of the bed and the gentle glow of the cave start to lull me into a state of relaxation.

"Thank you, Stripe," I whisper, my eyes already starting to close. He nods, a soft grunt of acknowledgment escaping his lips.

As I sink into the bed, my thoughts begin to blur, the surreal nature of everything fading into a comforting haze. Sleep pulls me under almost instantly, my body and mind surrendering to the much-needed rest.

The last thing I see is Stripe standing guard at the entrance, a silent protector in this hidden world. And then, darkness takes over, wrapping me in a deep, dreamless sleep.

Chapter Eight

I've just woken up and I feel like I've had the best sleep of my life. This moss bed is surprisingly comfortable. I was going to lie here a little longer, but I can hear something moving in the room. I'm not worried. It's probably Stripe again.

I pull back the curtains around the bed and peek out. Yup, it's Stripe. He's bringing more food.

"Hey Stripe," I say, stretching as I get out of bed. My muscles feel relaxed, and my mind is clear.

Stripe turns to look at me, his expression gentle.

Hello Emily. I have brought more food and water for you.

His voice is deep and resonant in my mind. It surprises me for a moment — I forgot about the telepathy thing.

"Thank you," I reply, genuinely grateful. "How long was I asleep?"

You were asleep for several hours. It is evening now.

I blink in surprise.

"Evening? Wow, I'm sorry for sleeping so long."

It is understandable. The magic in the ritual was likely a lot for a human to process.

I nod, realizing he's right. The ritual, the glowing water, the cum bath — it's all been overwhelming, but in a good way. I feel different, more connected to this place and these beings.

"Thank you, Stripe," I say again, reaching for the food he brought. "I really appreciate all of this."

He nods, his eyes softening.

You are welcome, Emily. We are glad to have you here.

I look down at myself and I realize I'm still wearing the towel from earlier, and it feels a bit silly standing here like this.

"Stripe, could you get my clothes from the pool?" I ask.

Stripe shakes his head gently.

You will not need your human clothes. The other Eldruk have woven a dress more fitting for a queen.

I'm not sure where to start unpacking that sentence. The "Eldruk" part I can guess — it's probably what the Bigfoot call themselves. It makes sense, why would they use the name we humans invented? But the "queen" part — that's a bit of a mystery.

I look at Stripe, searching his face for any sign that he's going to explain.

I will fetch your new dress, he says, turning to leave the room.

"Ok, great," I say, trying to sound casual. There's so much I don't understand yet, but I can feel the sincerity in Stripe's words. They've put a lot of thought into this, whatever it is.

As he disappears down the tunnel, I sit down and focus on my food. The meal is simple and nourishing, but I don't feel particularly hungry.

Stripe returns, holding a garment that takes my breath away. It's pale and shimmering, finely woven with an intricate swirling pattern. I reach out and touch it, feeling the soft, silky fabric under my fingertips.

"What is this made from?" I ask, my voice filled with wonder.

It is the silk of spiders, Stripe replies, his tone matter-of-fact.

"Spider silk?" I echo, skeptical. "But spider silk would be too weak."

Stripe smiles gently, a knowing look in his eyes.

You have much to learn about the natural world.

He places the dress carefully on the bed, the shimmering fabric catching the light.

Put this on. When you are ready, come out.

I nod, still in awe of the beautiful garment. Stripe leaves the room, and I can't help but run my fingers over the dress again. It's incredible, and the fact that it's made from spider silk adds another layer of mystery to this place. Humans could learn a lot from these beings.

I slip into the dress, the silky fabric cool against my skin. It fits perfectly, almost altering itself to fit my form. The texture is unlike anything I've ever worn, soft and strong at the same time. I feel almost ethereal, like I'm wearing a piece of the forest's magic.

Taking a deep breath, I head towards the entrance of my chamber. Just outside, Stripe is waiting for me. He looks at me and bows deeply.

You are most beautiful, my queen.

I blush, feeling warmth rise to my cheeks.

Stripe straightens up, his eyes meeting mine with a gentle warmth.

Kruk would like to speak with you, he says.

I blush again, remembering my swim with Kruk. My cheeks burn, and my stomach flips.

"Oh, okay," I manage to say, trying to sound casual again, but failing miserably.

Stripe gives me an encouraging nod.

He is waiting for you in his chamber.

As I follow Stripe down the glowing tunnels, my thoughts race. What does Kruk want to talk about? Is it to perform more rituals with me? More rituals involving his cock? The last one was over before I could even get involved...

Stripe and I pass through a large open chamber where a group of Eldruk are gathered. Some are weaving fabrics from spider silk, their large hands deftly handling the delicate threads. Others are tending to a garden of bioluminescent plants, their gentle glow lighting up the room. I count the individuals as we walk through. There can only be six to ten Bigfoot in total. This doesn't seem very many to me. But, to be fair, ten is way more than I thought existed until a few hours ago.

"How long have you lived here?" I ask Stripe, trying to absorb every detail.

For many generations, he replies, his voice reverberating in my mind. *We have learned to live in harmony with the earth.*

As we move deeper into the caverns, I notice how each area has its own purpose. There are chambers for sleeping, working, and even a communal space where the Bigfoot gather. The air is filled with a sense of calm and purpose, a stark contrast to the chaos of the outside world. I can't help but feel a deep respect for these beings. They have created a sanctuary here, hidden from the eyes of humanity, living in peace and unity.

We reach the entrance to a cavern that looks different from the others. Around the edges of the entrance are intricate carvings that tell stories I can't yet understand. I see a crude etching of a Bigfoot — its enormous phallus decorated in what I can only assume are veins. This must be Kruk's personal chamber.

Stripe pauses at the entrance and calls out, using his grunts and growls.

Deep inside my mind, a voice resonates, *Enter.*

The deep, sensual tone of Kruk's voice sends a jolt from my chest to between my legs. I look up at Stripe, a flutter of nervousness in my stomach. His smile is reassuring.

I will wait outside for you, he says, gesturing for me to go ahead.

Taking a deep breath, I step into the chamber. The walls are lined with more intricate carvings and glowing moss. The air feels heavy with history and power.

As I move deeper into the chamber, Kruk comes into view. Standing before me, he is even more imposing than I remembered from the pool. Taller, broader, his cock thicker and hanging almost to his knees. His fur is a deep shade of brown that glimmers slightly in the light of the moss. His eyes, thoughtful and intense, hold a wisdom that seems as old as the earth itself. He doesn't have striped patterns on his arms like Stripe. Instead, he is covered with larger splodges, like a calico cat. He's actually quite attractive, as crazy as that sounds. There's a strength in his features that is captivating.

"Kruk," I say softly, my voice echoing slightly in the cavernous room. He nods slightly, a welcoming gesture that makes my heart skip a beat.

I trust you slept well and your accommodation is to your liking?

"Yes, the room is wonderful, and the dress..." I pause, glancing down at the shimmering fabric, "it's beautiful. Thank you."

I'm not just being polite. I really am grateful.

Please, sit.

Kruk gestures to a seating area formed from smoothed stone, covered with layers of soft moss. I take a seat, feeling the cool moss beneath me. Kruk sits opposite, his large form gracefully lowering onto the mossy bench. I find myself studying him — the way the dim light plays across his fur, highlighting the muscular contours of his arms and chest. He looks so masculine, so inherently wild. And yet, his voice and manner possess a gentlemanly quality that intrigues me. How can a beast so terrifying, be so measured and polite?

Kruk studies me for a moment, his gaze thoughtful.

Do you have any questions?

"Actually, yes," I start, seizing the opportunity. "Stripe mentioned the word 'Eldruk'. What is that?"

Eldruk, Kruk begins, his eyes lighting up as if the story itself pleases him, ***is what we call ourselves. It is the name we have used since our ancient ancestors.***

I nod, absorbing his words.

"How ancient are the Eldruk? Where do your species come from?" I ask, my curiosity deepening.

We have been here as long as the forests themselves. Millennia have passed since the first Eldruk walked these lands. We have seen civilizations rise and fall, yet we remain hidden, part of the world but apart from its conflicts.

"Why stay hidden? There are thousands of humans who are waiting to meet you," I probe further, leaning in.

Because the world of humans is not ready for us. Fear and misunderstanding drive your kind. We seek to live in peace, without the threat of harm or exploitation.

As we talk, I find myself drawn into the rhythm of his speech, the thoughtful pauses, the way his eyes reflect a profound understanding of the world. There's a charisma about him that's hard to ignore, a charm that goes beyond his words.

"Have the Eldruk always lived underground?" I continue, intrigued.

Not always. The surface was once our home, but as human populations grew, we retreated beneath the earth. These caverns provide shelter and secrecy, elements vital for our survival.

The way Kruk describes his history, I find myself not just listening, but truly connecting with his story. It's as if every word weaves a deeper bond between us, pulling me into a world I never knew existed.

"And your people, the Eldruk," I say, "do you all possess the ability to communicate like this?" I tap my temple lightly, indicating the telepathic connection.

Yes. It is a gift of the Eldruk, one that strengthens our community and keeps us united.

As the conversation flows, I'm not just charmed; I'm enchanted. Kruk, with his blend of wisdom and warmth, seems more than just a leader of his people — he's a bridge to a forgotten world, and I'm standing at the threshold, captivated by every word.

As we continue talking, a thought strikes me.

"I've noticed I've only encountered male Eldruk. Are the females in another part of the caves?" I ask, scanning Kruk's face for a reaction.

Kruk's expression turns somber.

There are no females. They died out long ago due to a disease that afflicted only our kind.

My eyes widen in surprise.

"Then, how do you... I mean, how do the Eldruk reproduce?"

The question feels awkward as soon as I utter it, but my curiosity pushes me past the discomfort. Kruk hesitates, his eyes locking with mine.

This is why you are here, Emily.

I pause, confused.

"I don't understand. I'm human. I can't reproduce with the Eldruk."

There is a ritual. It was first performed by our ancestors when the lines between our kinds were not so strictly drawn. This ritual will enable you to carry our offspring.

Without meaning to, I accidentally glance down at Kruk's colossal dong.

I realize that we are... intimidating in that department. But I promise that the act of copulation will bring you nothing but extreme pleasure.

His emphasis on the words "extreme pleasure" creates a flutter in my stomach and I press my thighs together, trying to compose myself as he continues.

You witnessed the Eldruk mating in the woods and felt the primal pleasure resonate within you. This was no coincidence. It was a sign that you have been chosen. No one else would be able to handle the immense pleasure as you would.

I think back to what I witnessed in the woods. The way their heaving bodies entranced me. The uncontrollable lust that rose up within me. Is Kruk right? Am I the chosen one?

Emily, you will need to fully consent to this ritual. If you do not desire this position of pleasure, I will ensure your safe return to the human realm.

His voice is solemn, his gaze intense, ensuring I understand the choice is mine.

Be wary of your choice, Emily. If you choose to become the Eldruk queen, you cannot return to your old life. Once the ritual is complete, your decision is final. You will be bound to our world, our ways.

I have one more question to ask Kruk. I take a deep breath before asking, a little nervous as to what the answer might be.

"In this ritual, will you and I…"

Yes, Emily. During the ritual, you will take my cock inside you.

My core becomes wet instantly, and I already know my answer.

"Yes. I'll do it."

Kruk nods, a hint of relief in his expression.

The ritual will commence tomorrow at nightfall, in the forest under the full moon. It is there that the magic energies are strongest, vital for the ritual's power.

Well, fuck me. I just agreed to get railed by a sasquatch.

Chapter Nine

I pace around my room, unable to contain my impatience for nightfall. All day I have been aroused, desperate to rub one out, but I'm saving myself for Kruk and our moonlight ritual.

The throbbing sensation between my legs grows stronger with each passing minute. I'm desperately trying to ignore it but the thought of Kruk's colossal cock penetrating deep inside me is too much. Fuck it, I can cum twice in one day.

I slip a hand under my spider silk dress and slide my fingers along my slick folds. I shudder at the contact, stroking myself faster. I'm so close. I'm right on the edge.

Wait, is that footsteps?

I whip my hand back and smooth my dress.

Stripe stands in the doorway, his eyes seeming to glow in the dim light. He tilts his head back, nostrils flaring as he inhales deeply. A rumbling growl emanates from his broad chest and his lips pull back, revealing sharp white teeth in a predatory grin.

I can smell your desire, my queen, he says, his cock swelling ever so slightly. ***But you must wait for your king.***

Tonight, Kruk will fill you with his seed until your womb swells with new life.

My breath catches at his words and my body clenches in anticipation. He's right, I need to wait. Tonight, I am Kruk's.

Just then, Kruk appears in my chamber. His fur is adorned with intricate gold markings. They appear to be some kind of runes. His manhood, already semi-erect, is frighteningly large.

Are you ready, Emily?

I nod mutely, unable to form words as I take in the sight of him. He extends a hand towards me, and I place my trembling one in his warm palm.

We make our way through the dimly lit tunnels of the Eldruk territory until, in the distance, I see moonlight. We continue walking until the underground passageway opens onto a glade in the Payette National Forest. A silvery glow bathes the clearing, cast by the full moon above. The trees around the clearing seem to sway in time with my racing heartbeat, their leaves rustling like whispers of excitement. I can feel the Eldruk's eyes on us, their presence electric in the air. There is no turning back now.

A sacred circle has been laid on the ground, at its edges I can see intricate runes that glow with an ethereal blue. Kruk leads me into the center. He turns to face me, his eyes burning with a primal fire that both terrifies and arouses me. His hand trembles ever so slightly as he brushes a lock of hair from my face, tucking it behind my ear.

Are you sure you want this, Emily? he asks, his voice husky with barely restrained desire. *Once we begin the ritual, there is no turning back.*

I take a deep breath, my heart pounding in my chest.

"I'm sure."

Relief and lust mingle in his eyes as he nods.

Very well. Lay down.

I comply, the ground is soft against my back. Kruk kneels between my legs. Slowly, he trails one claw down my body, slicing through the fabric of my gown. I gasp as the scraps of white material fall away, leaving me exposed.

Kruk's eyes devour my naked form hungrily.

So beautiful.

He runs his hands along my inner thighs, parting them. I whimper in anticipation.

The Eldruk stand around us now, forming a circle, their feral eyes fixated on our every move. I can feel their lust and anticipation as if it were my own.

With a primal growl, Kruk's beastly form takes over completely. He rears back on his hind legs and roars. His massive cock, now fully erect, juts out from his hairy abdomen, glistening in the moonlight. It's even more monstrous than I could have imagined, easily the size of my forearm, if not bigger. A thick line of precum oozes from the swollen purple head, tinting the air with its musky scent.

Lifting his hulking form over me, Kruk lowers himself carefully onto all fours. His mass is astounding, but I feel no pain as his clawed paws support his immense body. He brings his muzzle close to my face, our noses touching.

Tonight, I claim you as mine.

A deep-rooted part of me thrills at the idea of being claimed by this magnificent beast. I nod vigorously in agreement, my heart pounding in anticipation.

The Eldruk around the edges begin to sing again, their haunting voices echoing through the forest. The melody is primal, ancient — it seeps into my bones and resonates deep within my core. Kruk's claws trail down my sides, his eyes burning with feral intensity as he gazes upon my naked form.

My breath catches in my throat as I feel the tip of his cock brush against my entrance. I am helpless, surrendering myself fully to the ritual and the beast above me. Slowly, agonizingly, Kruk pushes forward, stretching me wider than I ever thought possible. I cry out, back arching, toes curling into the soft earth beneath me. It won't fit. There's no way I can take it.

Kruk begins to sing too, his deep baritone joining the haunting chorus of the Eldruk. The melody seems to emanate from his very soul. His voice reverberates through my body as he continues his slow advance, filling me deeper and deeper with his mighty dick. I gasp and moan, overcome by the intensity of the sensation. My inner walls stretch to accommodate him, slick heat enveloping inch after inch of his throbbing shaft. Above me, Kruk's expression is one of ecstasy, his eyes glowing with fiery possession.

The singing swells, voices intertwine in a hypnotic tapestry of sound. Kruk draws back slowly before thrusting forward once more, eliciting a strangled cry from my lips. He sets a steady rhythm, each powerful stroke going deeper than the last. I cling to his fur desperately, lost in a haze of pleasure.

There is a flash of pain as my body struggles to accommodate his girth, then an overwhelming sense of fullness as Kruk sheaths himself fully inside me. We are connected now, beast and woman, our energies mingling and coalescing. The Eldruk's song crescendos, fueling the primal magic that binds us. Kruk begins to move, rocking his hips in an ancient rhythm. With each powerful thrust, he touches something deep within me, a part of my soul I never knew existed.

The Eldruk's song shifts, the tempo increasing to match our frenzied coupling. Kruk's eyes blaze with feral lust as he pounds into me, my body rocking beneath him. I'm lost in ecstasy, tossed about on waves of pleasure so intense they border on pain. My fingers tangle in Kruk's thick fur, holding on for dear life. His hot breath gusts against my neck and shoulders as he drives into me over and over. I can feel every ridge and vein of his monstrous cock stretching my tight passage.

The Eldruk's song reaches a fever pitch, their voices rising to a crescendo that seems to tear at the very fabric of reality itself. The runes etched into the ground beneath us glow brighter, casting shimmering lights that dance across our entangled bodies like phantom lovers. An incredible heat begins to build deep inside me, coalescing in my womb, and I know that the time has come.

I claim thee as mine.

"And I thee," I manage to gasp in response, my voice hoarse with need. "I claim you as my own."

As our climax approaches, I can feel the ancient magic uncoiling inside me like a coiled snake, seeking release. The runes around us glow brighter still, casting strange shadows on our entwined bodies. The very air seems to vibrate with power.

Bound body and soul. Through space and time, I am yours. I accept your claim.

As the words resonate in my mind, the world seems to explode into a kaleidoscope of colors. The forest around us shimmers and warps, as if it were no more than a reflection on the surface of a pond. The Eldruk's cries of ecstasy reach an ear-splitting pitch, their forms blurring into one undulating mass of energy.

The orgasm hits me like a freight train, tearing through every fiber of my being. I arch my back, my nails digging into Kruk's fur as wave after wave of pleasure washes over me. His gargantuan cock pulsates deep inside me. His hot seed fills me in long, powerful spurts. I feel a searing heat in my core as if my very essence is being rewritten.

As our orgasms subside, the world around us begins to settle. The ripples in the fabric of reality calm. The runes on the ground fade away, leaving no trace of their existence. The other

Eldruk disperse into the trees, leaving Kruk and me alone in the clearing.

Kruk withdraws from me slowly, and I whimper at the feeling of emptiness that washes over me.

It is done. The ritual is complete.

Slowly, I sit up, my body aching in places I didn't know existed. My eyes meet Kruk's, and in them, I see a depth of emotion that takes my breath away.

We are now bound, he says quietly in my mind. **From this day forth, we are one.**

I nod, unable to find words to express the connection I feel with him at this moment.

In the flickering light of the forest, just over Kruk's shoulder, I see a figure in the shadows. I assume it's a lingering Eldruk, I barely give it a second glance until a trembling voice cuts through the night air.

"Emily?"

My heart stops. That voice. I know that voice. I turn, my stomach clenching with sudden dread. It's Mark, my boyfriend.

Horror washes over me as I see the confusion and fear in his eyes. He steps out into the clearing, looking between me and Kruk.

"What are you doing?" he asks, his voice shaking.

Fuck, how am I going to explain this?

Chapter Ten

Mark looks horrified, his eyes wide as he stares at Kruk. What should I do? I'm torn between running to him and staying by Kruk's side.

Kruk shifts into protector mode, positioning himself between me and Mark. He growls; a deep, rumbling sound that vibrates through the air. He stands taller, his muscles tensing, claws unsheathing with a menacing click. Mark steps back, his face pale, clearly thinking Kruk is about to attack.

"Kruk, no! Don't hurt him!" I cry out, my voice sharp with panic.

Kruk turns his head slightly to look at me, his eyes intense.

Do you know this human?

"Yes, I know him. He's... he is my boyfriend," I explain quickly, my words tumbling out.

Kruk's brow furrows in confusion.

Boyfriend?

"He was my mate," I clarify, hoping this word will make more sense to him.

Kruk's posture relaxes slightly, but he remains alert, protective. He glances at Mark again, assessing, then looks back at me.

"Kruk, he's not a threat," I add earnestly, hoping to ease the tension before it escalates further.

I turn toward Mark, my heart aching. I didn't want him to find me like this, to find out about my new life at all.

"It's ok, Mark," I say, trying to reassure him. But let's be real, he just watched me get pummeled in the pussy by a Bigfoot. There's not much I can say or do to calm this situation.

Mark stares at me, confusion and fear etched across his face. His voice trembles as he speaks.

"Emily, have you gone crazy? I just caught you fucking a monster. Nothing is ok. And now you're talking to it like it understands you!"

Oh yeah. I forgot that Mark can't hear their telepathy. I probably look a little nuts right now.

I take a deep breath, trying to maintain my composure under his worried gaze.

"Mark, the Eldruk speak telepathically. They can understand more than you think."

Mark's eyebrows knit together, and he takes a step back. The idea of telepathic communication was possibly a step too far.

"Telepathy? Emily, are you serious? This sounds insane."

I can see the wheels turning in his head, his rational mind grappling with the surreal situation. He looks from me to Kruk, who stands calmly, watching our exchange with an intense focus.

"Mark, I know how this looks. But I promise I'm not crazy," I insist, my voice steady despite the rising panic I feel at his skepticism. "I've been living with them, learning from them. Please, just try to understand."

"Learning how to take 20-inch dick apparently!"

I rub my hands over my forehead. This conversation isn't going well at all.

"Mark, please," I beg, "just give me a minute to speak with Kruk and then I'll explain everything."

Mark shakes his head, clearly struggling to accept what I'm saying.

I turn back to Kruk, seeking his permission.

"Can I have some time to speak with Mark alone?" I ask, hoping he understands the necessity.

Kruk nods slowly.

Yes, it is only fair that you resolve any matters from your human life. But the forest is not safe for such discussions. We should take him into the tunnels.

I nod in agreement, relieved by his understanding.

Turning back to Mark, I see he's still visibly shaken. As I approach, Mark drapes his jacket over my shoulders, and I realize I'm still naked from the ritual. Kruk's seed is dribbling down my legs.

"Mark," I start, my voice soft but firm, "I want to explain everything to you, but not here. It's not safe, and it's complicated." I gesture toward the shadowy outlines of the tunnel entrance. "Please, come with us. I'll tell you everything on the way."

Mark hesitates, his gaze shifting between me and the looming figure of Kruk behind me. He looks back into my eyes, searching for the Emily he knows. After a tense moment, he sees whatever it is he needs to see.

"Okay, Emily," he finally says, his voice low. "I'll come with you. I don't understand all this, but I trust you."

Relief washes over me. I reach out, taking his hand.

"Thank you, Mark," I say as we start walking towards the tunnels. "I promise, I'll explain everything as best as I can."

As we enter the shadows of the Eldruk territory, I squeeze his hand. Despite everything, it is good to see him again.

Together we follow Kruk into the deep, shadowy tunnels. The air cools, and the soft glow of moss lights our path. I take a deep breath, readying myself to explain the unbelievable.

"They're called Eldruk," I start, "that's what they call themselves. What we know as Bigfoot or Sasquatch."

Mark's steps falter slightly as he processes this.

"Eldruk," he repeats slowly, testing the word.

"Yes," I nod, continuing. "They're not monsters, Mark. They're intelligent, kind, nature-loving creatures. They live here, underground, away from human eyes."

As we walk, I point out small details in the tunnel — the way the moss is cultivated, the gentle architecture of the paths, and the occasional glimpse of an Eldruk moving in the distance. As

I introduce Mark to their world, I can see his terror gradually morphing into fascination.

"This... It's incredible, Em," he admits. "They've built all this?"

"Yes," I say. "They have their own society, their own culture. It's complex and beautiful."

"And they speak through telepathy?" he asks, a hint of skepticism still lingering.

"They do," I confirm. "That's how Kruk and I have been communicating."

"So how come I can't hear them?" he asks.

I think back to the ceremony in the pool. The torrent of jizz slapping me in the face.

"You have to partake in a special ritual," I explain carefully, "it's not just something they let any human do."

Thankfully, Mark doesn't press for more information about the telepathy ritual. Instead, he looks around, trying to imagine the invisible conversations happening all around him.

"It's a lot to take in," he says.

"It is," I agree, giving him a reassuring smile. "But I'm here to help you through it. Just keep an open mind."

He nods, and we continue walking, his grip on my hand a little tighter.

The three of us arrive at my underground bedroom. Kruk stops at the entrance, his large frame filling the doorway.

I will give you the night to finish your personal business with the human realm, Kruk announces, his voice echoing in my mind. ***But tomorrow he must leave.***

"Thank you, Kruk. I understand," I respond gratefully.

Kruk nods solemnly and then turns to leave.

Mark and I enter my chamber. It's quiet. I release a breath I didn't realize I was holding and turn to face Mark.

"Okay," I say, offering him a small, tentative smile. "Let's talk."

Mark takes a deep breath, his eyes searching the chamber before settling back on me.

"I thought you had died, Emily," he begins, his voice cracking slightly. "When you didn't answer any calls, I... I drove out to the forest."

He pauses, swallowing hard, his hands trembling slightly.

"I found your campervan. It was ruined, like maybe a bear had attacked it." His voice wavers as if he might cry, but then he steadies himself, drawing in a slow, deep breath. "I'm so glad you're alive. After our argument, I could never have forgiven myself if something had happened to you."

I listen to his story, taking it in. But inside, I feel detached. Since the ritual, since meeting the Eldruk, I haven't thought of Mark or our argument at all. It hadn't even crossed my mind that he would be worried. His presence, his concern — it all makes me realize just how far I've drifted from my old life in such a short time. I'm committed to this new path, so much so that I didn't spare a thought for those I left behind.

"I'm sorry, Mark," I say quietly, my voice sincere. "I didn't think... I didn't realize you'd be so worried. I've been through a lot here, and it's changed everything for me."

Mark nods, looking both relieved to see me and overwhelmed by the enormity of the situation.

"I can see that, Em. This place, it's like nothing I ever imagined. But I'm just glad you're safe. That's all that matters now."

I look at Mark. Sweet, stupid Mark. I need to be honest with him.

"Mark, there's something important you need to know. I am part of an ancient prophecy to become the Eldruk queen."

Mark's eyes widen.

"Is that why you were fucking Mr. Long-Cock in the woods?" he asks, trying to piece everything together.

"Yes," I reply. "That ritual was part of it."

Mark frowns, a look of concern crossing his face.

"Emily, are you sure they haven't put some kind of spell on you? What if you're not really in control of your mind?"

I shake my head firmly.

"Although there is magic here, the Eldruk haven't put any spell on me. Everything I've done, everything I'm doing, is of my own accord. I chose this path after understanding what it meant."

Mark pauses, absorbing my words. His eyes fill with tears again, the realization of what I'm trying to say dawning on him.

"You're not coming back with me to the human world, are you?" His voice is a whisper, barely audible.

"No, Mark, I'm not coming back. My place is here now, with the Eldruk. This is my path."

Silence hangs between us as he processes the finality of my decision. I can see the pain and acceptance battling within him. Just then, Stripe enters the chamber, his arms full of wood for the fire. The sudden appearance of the large Eldruk makes Mark flinch slightly, but I give him a reassuring look.

"Thank you, Stripe," I say as he carefully places the wood down, fueling the small blaze that casts warm, flickering light around us.

Stripe takes a long look at Mark.

I find this human very attractive. His form is pleasing to me. I see why you chose him as your mate.

Mark catches my eye, a wary expression on his face.

"Is the beast using his mind powers on me?" he asks.

I frown slightly at his choice of words.

"No, but he is talking to me telepathically," I reply. "But please, call him Stripe, not 'beast'. He's not a monster."

Mark nods, swallowing his discomfort.

"What did he say?"

"He said he finds you very attractive and understands why you and I were a couple," I translate, watching as Stripe stands quietly by, observing our interaction.

Mark looks Stripe up and down, taking in his imposing form.

"Attractive, huh?"

I reach out and touch Mark's arm gently.

"Don't worry, Mark. Consent is very important here. You don't have to do anything you don't want to."

Mark takes a moment to really look at Stripe, his eyes scanning the Eldruk from head to toe. I notice Mark's eyes linger on Stripe's thick member for just a moment too long. Then, unexpectedly, a blush creeps into Mark's cheeks.

"I mean, I can kind of see the allure," he admits, almost reluctantly.

I laugh lightly at his comment, pleased by his shift in perspective.

"They are quite something to behold, aren't they?" I say, my eyes glancing over to Stripe.

"Thank you, Stripe, for bringing the wood. That was very thoughtful."

Stripe nods, then takes one last curious look at Mark before he turns to leave the chamber.

As soon as Stripe exits, Mark puts his head in his hands, his shoulders slumping visibly. The day's revelations and the emotional rollercoaster seem to have finally caught up with him. He looks utterly exhausted.

"Mark, you should sleep a while," I suggest gently, touching his arm to offer some comfort.

He looks up at me, weariness etched across his face. Without a word, he nods and slowly lies down on the moss bed. It doesn't take long before his eyes flutter shut, and he drifts off to sleep. I watch him for a few minutes, observing the steady rise and fall of his chest. The tension on his face eases as he slips deeper into sleep.

While Mark sleeps, I think I'll take a little midnight trip to Kruk's chamber. It's a sort of wedding night, after all, and we all know what couples do on their wedding night...

Chapter Eleven

I head back to my chamber after a night of frenzied fucking with Kruk. I feel surprisingly well rested considering how many times we banged. Who knew ancient beings could be so talented in bed? I hope Mark slept well. He'll need his strength today for his return home.

As I approach my chamber door, a strange sound catches my ear. Muffled grunts and wet smacking drift through the tunnel. I pause, tilting my head to listen. The noises quicken, sounding almost frantic.

I pause. My heart begins to race. What is Mark doing in there?

I approach the chamber quietly, not wanting to disturb whatever is happening inside. Carefully, I turn the corner and peek into the room.

There on my bed lies Stripe, his massive furry body taking up nearly the entire mattress. His thick cock stands upright, throbbing and glistening. Kneeling before him is Mark, desperately licking and sucking the Eldruk's enormous shaft.

I gasp softly at the sight. Mark's eyes are glazed over with lust, his focus entirely consumed by pleasuring Stripe's cock. He seems almost possessed, stroking himself feverishly as he works his tongue up and down the veiny length. Drool drips from his chin as he struggles to fit the head in his mouth, grunting with exertion. My eyes flick to Stripe. He lies relaxed amidst the moss, one clawed hand gently guiding Mark's movements. His golden eyes find mine, and he grins knowingly. I feel my cheeks flush, arousal beginning to stir between my legs.

"Well, well," I purr, sauntering into the room. Mark jerks his head toward me, eyes wide.

"Don't stop on my account," I say, feeling a wicked grin spread across my face.

I crawl onto the bed, sidling up next to Mark.

"Let me help you with that," I murmur, grasping Stripe's enormous girth with both hands.

My fingers meet just below the head of Stripe's cock, teasing the sensitive underside, causing him to moan in delight. Mark looks over at me, his eyes glazed over with lust but also filled with an apology.

"It's alright," I say, winking at him. "The Eldruk are pretty irresistible."

Together, we work on either side of Stripe's shaft, our tongues sliding up and down the veiny length in tandem. The taste of Stripe's musk is intoxicating, a heady mix of pine and aggression that arouses Mark and mine's primal urges further. Mark moans as he sucks on the head of Stripe's cock, his own erection straining.

"Let me take care of you too," I whisper. I slide my hand down Mark's abs and grasp his hard length. He gasps, bucking into my hand. I stroke him firmly as I continue licking Stripe's shaft.

"Yes, just like that," Mark groans through gritted teeth. Pre-cum beads at the tip of his cock.

Stripe rumbles approvingly, his massive body undulating. I feel his claws gently comb through my hair. The primal energy in the room builds. We are all connected in this frenzy of lust.

As Mark's arousal grows, I can sense Stripe's desire growing as well. The Eldruk lets out a low growl, his golden eyes boring into me.

Tell the human I wish to take him fully.

I pause, leaning in to whisper Stripe's request into Mark's ear. Mark's eyes go wide, and he looks between Stripe and me with apprehension and excitement.

"Are...are you sure?" Mark asks hesitantly.

I nod, giving him a reassuring smile.

"Don't worry, I'll be here to guide you," I tell Mark.

Mark takes a deep breath and nods.

"Okay. I want this."

I grin, pleased that Mark is opening himself to new experiences. I help Mark onto his hands and knees before Stripe, angling his hips up enticingly. Stripe wastes no time, grasping Mark's waist with his huge hands.

I watch intently as Stripe extends his long, rough tongue and slides it up the cleft of Mark's asscheeks. Mark lets out a surprised whimper at the warm, wet sensation. Stripe continues to lap slowly, thoroughly coating Mark's most private area with thick saliva.

"Mmm yes, get him nice and wet," I purr encouragingly.

Mark grips the moss bed, overcome by the new pleasures assaulting him. Stripe works his tongue in practiced circles, teasing Mark's tight hole. A low groan escapes Mark's throat when the tip of Stripe's tongue finally breaches his entrance. Stripe grunts in satisfaction at Mark's reaction, grasping his hips more firmly as he works his tongue deeper inside.

"Oh god," Mark gasps, his thighs quivering.

Stripe's thick, dexterous tongue explores Mark's tight passage, coaxing muffled cries of ecstasy from the man. I continue stroking Mark's straining cock, precum now dripping freely down the swollen head.

But wait, I have an idea... I position myself beneath Mark, laying back and spreading my legs wide. My slick pussy glistens in the firelight, ready and waiting to receive him. I reach down and use my fingers to spread my soft pink folds, exposing my aching clit. Mark looks down at me with lust-blown eyes, his body trembling from the pleasure of Stripe's talented tongue. He slowly pulls himself away from the Eldruk's ministrations, a thin trail of saliva still connecting them.

Stripe's eyes blaze as he watches Mark move between my open thighs. Mark's cock bobs heavily, the engorged head shiny with precum. He holds the base of his shaft, guiding it to my slick entrance. We both moan deeply as he presses inside me. Behind him, Stripe positions his massive erection at Mark's slick hole. Mark tenses in anticipation, letting out a shuddering breath.

"Go slow," I whisper to Stripe.

The Eldruk nods. He rubs the tip of his cock against Mark's entrance, coating it with precum. Mark whimpers, pushing back against him. Stripe begins to press forward, breaching Mark's tight ring of muscle. Mark cries out, his body stretching to accommodate Stripe's enormous girth. I reach up to caress Mark soothingly as inch by inch, Stripe's length disappears inside him.

"Oh god, you feel so good," Mark groans. "So full..."

Stripe grunts approvingly, sliding deeper still until finally he is buried to the hilt in Mark's tight heat. Mark pants heavily, adjusted now to the intense stretch and fullness.

Slowly, Stripe begins to move, pulling back before pushing forward again. Each thrust nudges Mark deeper into me, and I moan at the increased pressure against my swollen pussy. Together, we moved as one, a writhing mass of muscle and fur. A sexual Victoria sponge cake.

"Oh fuck," Mark moans, his voice raw with pleasure as Stripe's massive girth stretches him open. "I've never... felt any thing... like this."

I moan in agreement, my nails digging into the moss beneath me

"Yes... Just like that," I pant, my breath coming in ragged gasps. "Fuck me... Fuck us both..."

I can feel my climax building. Pressure mounting inside, ready to erupt. Mark's eyes are squeezed shut, his face etched with pleasure-pain as Stripe's massive shaft plunges into him over and over.

"I'm close," Mark gasps through gritted teeth. His thighs tremble where they bracket my hips. I reach between us and rub tight circles around my aching clit, my pussy clenching hungrily on Mark's driving cock.

"Let go," I urge them both. "Cum for me."

Stripe tosses back his head and roars, the guttural sound primal and raw. His claws dig into Mark's hips as his rhythm grows faster, more frenzied. Mark cries out wordlessly, spurred on by the building crescendo of our passion. I feel Mark swell and pulse inside me as his orgasm takes over. Hot, thick jets of cum fill me up, triggering my own shattering climax. My back arches up off the bed as waves of pleasure crash through me.

Mark collapses onto me, utterly spent and exhausted. His body trembles with aftershocks as he struggles to catch his breath. But Stripe isn't finished yet. With a grunt, he pulls his massive cock free from Mark's stretched hole. Stripe then uses one huge hand to gently roll Mark's limp body off of me. I gasp as Mark's softening cock slips free of my dripping pussy. Stripe's eyes gleam hungrily as he takes in my prone, pleasure-wracked form beneath him.

Stripe hooks his arms under my knees and lifts my lower body up off the bed. I moan as the new position causes Mark's cum to leak from my throbbing pussy. Stripe rubs the swollen purple head of his cock through my soaked folds, coating himself in the slick evidence of Mark's release. Then he begins to press into me, my walls stretching impossibly wide around his massive girth. I cry out, lost in a haze of pain and pleasure.

Stripe fucks me over and over. Each plunge sends ripples of pleasure radiating through my core. The pleasure builds again within me, rising higher and higher until my climax crashes over me like a tidal wave. I screamed Stripe's name as my pussy spasms and clenches around his driving cock. Stripe roars as my pulsing inner walls milk his shaft. With a final brutal thrust, he slams into me, up to the hilt, and holds himself there as his cock erupts. Blast after blast of hot cum floods my womb until it can hold no more. Our combined juices overflow, trickling down my thighs and pooling on the moss beneath me.

Stripe slowly pulls out, his member dripping with our combined juices. He gives me a satisfied grunt as he collapses onto the bed alongside Mark and me.

I curl up between my two lovers, utterly spent and satisfied. Mark stirs beside me, wrapping an arm around my waist and nuzzling into my neck.

"That was incredible," he murmurs. "I've never felt anything like that before."

Stripe grunts in agreement, pressing his furry body against my back. His arms come around to envelop both Mark and me in his warm embrace.

I sigh contentedly, basking in the afterglow. I can't imagine anything more wonderful than being here with the Eldruk, experiencing intimacy and passion beyond anything I've ever known.

My old life seems so far away now. The world outside these walls doesn't exist anymore. All that matters is this new family.

Chapter Twelve

Mark and I stand at the entrance to the Eldruk tunnels, the midday sun is high overhead. The air is thick with the scent of pine and earth — a sharp contrast to the cool, muted world of the tunnels behind us.

Mark looks down at me, eyes filled with a mix of emotions.

"Emily, I'm sorry," he begins, his voice thick. "I didn't believe you about the Bigfoot. I should have trusted you more."

I shake my head gently, reaching out to touch his arm.

"Mark, no apology is needed. The past is the past."

He nods, but I can see the effort it takes for him to accept my reassurance.

"I've seen so much now," he continues. "Felt so much. I understand why you need to do this. Your destiny... It's incredible, Emily. And I'm... I'm really proud of you."

His words warm my heart.

"Thank you, Mark. That means a lot to me." I pause, gathering my thoughts. "You've been a huge part of my life. Becoming the Eldruk queen... it changes a lot for me, but it doesn't change what we've had. I want you to know that."

Mark's eyes soften, and he pulls me into a hug. It's a strong, warm embrace.

"I know, Em. And I respect you so much for taking this on. Just promise me you'll be careful."

"I promise," I whisper.

We stand there for a moment longer, holding onto the past for just a minute more. Finally, we step back. Mark looks at me once more, his gaze lingering as if memorizing my face.

"Take care of yourself, Em. And if you ever need anything..."

"I know where to find you," I finish for him, offering a small, bittersweet smile.

He nods, gives me one last look filled with love, then turns and walks away. I watch him go. There is no sadness, no regret. Only the feeling of resolute strength, knowing I am making the right choice.

Kruk appears at the entrance just as Mark disappears from view. We don't speak at first; he simply nods to me, and we turn together to walk back into the cool shadows of the tunnels. As we move through the dimly lit passageways, our footsteps echo softly off the walls. The air is cool and smells of earth and moss. It's a scent I've come to associate with safety and a new beginning.

"Kruk," I begin, my voice echoing slightly, "were you jealous of the time I spent with Mark and Stripe?"

It's a question that's been nagging at me all morning, a worry about how the dynamics within the Eldruk might work.

Kruk glances at me, his expression unreadable for a moment before he replies.

Not at all. In fact, as queen, you are expected to spend time mating with each Eldruk. It is necessary for the harmony and unity of our community.

His response brings a wave of relief, washing away the small tendrils of concern that had started to form.

"I'm glad to hear that," I reply, my steps feeling lighter. "I want to be a good leader for the Eldruk, to really be a part of this community."

Kruk nods, his eyes meeting mine in the dim light.

You are already well on your way, Emily. Stripe has already been telling the other Eldruk how transformative you were during his mating with you and Mark. The others are eager to experience your pleasure.

Hearing his words, a flush of excitement warms my cheeks. The idea that I could be railed by each and every Eldruk is thrilling.

Kruk leads me deeper into the network of tunnels until we arrive at a grand cave. The space opens up dramatically, the ceiling arching high above. The floor beneath our feet is completely covered in a thick layer of soft moss, cushioning our steps.

"What room is this?" I ask, my voice hushed in awe as I gaze around at the natural majesty of the place.

This, Kruk begins, spreading his arms wide as he turns to me, *is the group mating chamber. It is here where all the*

Eldruk can enjoy the pleasures of their queen together at the same time.

"Can we do that now?" I ask, eager to experience the hairy fuck pile of ten Eldruk all at once.

Kruk nods. There is a hint of pleasure in his expression.

Yes, we can, he confirms.

Kruk raises his voice, a deep, resonant call that echoes through the caverns, reaching out to the other Eldruk. I watch in awe as, one by one, they begin to enter the grand cave. They move with quiet dignity, their eyes on me, filled with a mixture of respect and arousal.

I step into the center of the chamber, feeling the moss soft under my feet. The Eldruk form a circle around me, their presence imposing yet comforting. I take a deep breath, gathering my thoughts and my courage.

"My lovers," I start, my voice steady and clear, reverberating off the stone walls. "I am deeply honored to stand here before you today."

The Eldruk watch me, attentive and silent, encouraging me to continue.

"I came to your world not knowing the full path I was destined to walk," I continue, my voice growing stronger with each word. "But now, I stand before you, ready to embrace this role, ready to learn, and be filled by your seed."

I pause, looking around at the faces in the crowd, seeing nods of approval and smiles of encouragement.

"With your guidance, I hope to bear many Eldruk children. I am committed to your kind for as long as I am able."

I take another breath, feeling a tingle between my thighs.

"I am here to serve your cocks, to grow fat with child, and to unite. Let us move forward together now, our bodies humming in the primal dance."

The chamber fills with a soft murmuring of approval. Kruk steps forward, his cock beginning to twitch.

You speak well, Emily. You are truly one of us now, he says, his voice filled with pride.

The air in the cavern is thick with anticipation and hunger. The other Eldruk begin to stir, their massive cocks swinging heavily between their hairy thighs, hardening with each passing moment. Knowing they are here for me, for my royal pussy — it's almost too much to bear.

Kruk is the first to step forward, his amber eyes locked on mine as he approaches. He doesn't say a word. He doesn't need to; his intentions are clear. I stand tall, bracing myself for what comes next.

He places a rough hand on my hip and guides me to all fours, positioning me so that my ass is in the air, my slit exposed and glistening with anticipation. With one strong thrust, Kruk buries himself deep inside me, filling me to the hilt. I gasp at the sudden intrusion. He's rougher than he has been before, but not careless. His movements are deep and primal as he claims me, marking me as his queen.

The sound of our mating fills the cavern, my moans intermingling with his primal growls. The others, unable to resist any longer, began to couple around us, their bodies moving with a frenzied rhythm.

"Oh, yes!" I moan as Kruk pounds into me relentlessly, his grizzly cock stretching me wide.

Behind me, I feel another Eldruk take my ass. They both work me in a rough but exquisite tango of pleasure as they vie for dominance, driving me higher and higher.

I look around the cavern and see more Eldruk joining in, pairs and then trios forming as they fuck on the mossy floor or against the stone walls. The sound of fur and flesh slapping against each other fills the air as they all succumb to their primal lusts. They are beautiful in their abandonment.

I close my eyes and sink into the pleasure coursing through my body. With Kruk behind me and the other Eldruk pounding forcefully into my ass, I am utterly overcome by sensation. They work in tandem, thrusting hard and deep. My moans echo off the cavern walls, harmonizing with the guttural grunts of the Eldruk surrounding me.

Just when I think I can't take any more, Kruk lets out a thunderous roar. He empties himself inside me. The smaller Eldruk follows close behind with his own climax. They withdraw. I am full of seed but I must have more.

I look up to see another Eldruk approaching. He gazes down at me, desire burning in his eyes. I rise to meet him, pressing my body against his muscular frame. He wraps his burly arms around me and lifts me effortlessly, spearing me onto his engorged member. My legs wrap around his waist. He begins to move, his powerful thrusts rocking my entire body as he fucks me hard and mercilessly.

Around us the orgy continues unabated, a swirling mass of writhing fur and unrestrained lust. The musk of sex hangs heavy in the air as the Eldruk rut without inhibition. Their stamina seems endless as they switch partners and positions, an endless parade of tongues, cocks, and claws. I am passed between them, never empty for long as one after another takes me hard. My moans turn into screams of ecstasy, and my thighs are soaked with the evidence of their desire. I am not a passive fuck toy – I am the object of their desire. A treasure much coveted.

I find myself with Kruk again. He lies beneath me, his tree-trunk thighs spread wide. I lower myself onto him, impaling myself on his girth. I am in charge. I take whoever's cock I want.

The air fills with the familiar static electricity — the Eldruk magic is palpable around me. I feel powerful. I feel alive.

"I am your queen," I call out, breathless with lust. "I am your queen, and my cunt is the altar at which you will worship. Fuck me, fill me, worship your queen!"

The static energy in the air intensifies. Their magic courses through me, igniting every nerve ending as our bodies collide in a frenzy of lust and magic.

I am Queen. I am Mother Nature herself.

Chapter Thirteen

Five Years Later

In the grand cavern, I sit upon my throne. My majestic seat is carved from an ancient tree that seems to have grown from the very heart of the earth. Its gnarled roots twist around my feet. Above my head, a headdress of intertwined branches and vibrant flowers crowns me. There is no mistaking me as Queen.

Beneath the luminous canopy of bioluminescent moss, young Eldruk play happily on the soft moss-covered floor. Their laughter echoes through the cavern. Over the years, I have birthed many beautiful, healthy Eldruk — both boys and girls. After all, that was why I was brought here — to help repopulate the colony, to ensure its survival and prosperity.

As I watch the young Eldruk play, Stripe enters. I point to a young female Eldruk, she is no older than two years old.

"That one," I say.

Stripe nods, understanding. He picks up the female gently, his large hands careful and precise.

"Kill it," I command.

As you wish, my queen.

He turns and leaves with the young Eldruk, his steps echoing solemnly.

I remain seated, my expression composed. It's a harsh decree, but necessary. There were no females when I arrived here, and now there are many. I alone am Queen. None shall usurp my crown.

In the shadows of the great tree, I sit — a queen both revered and feared. A protector who nurtures, culls, and fucks.